By D. R. Shealy

Illustrated by Erik Doescher, Mike DeCarlo, and David Tanguay

A Random House PICTUREBACK® Book
Random House 🏠 New York

DC SUPER FRIENDS and all related titles, characters, and elements are trademarks of DC Comics. Copyright © 2010 DC Comics. All rights reserved. Published in the United States by Golden Books, an imprint of Random House Children's Books, a division of Random House, Inc., 1745 Broadway, New York, NY 10019, and in Canada by Random House of Canada Limited, Toronto. Pictureback, Random House, and the Random House colophon are registered trademarks of Random House, Inc.

Library of Congress Control Number: 2009936081

ISBN: 978-0-375-84747-9

www.randomhouse.com/kids

Printed in the United States of America

10 9 8 7 6 5 4 3 2 1

The Batmobile screeched to a stop. Batman and Robin were responding to a Super Friends distress signal in Gotham City. The Flash and Cyborg arrived moments later. "Where are the other Super Friends?" Robin asked.

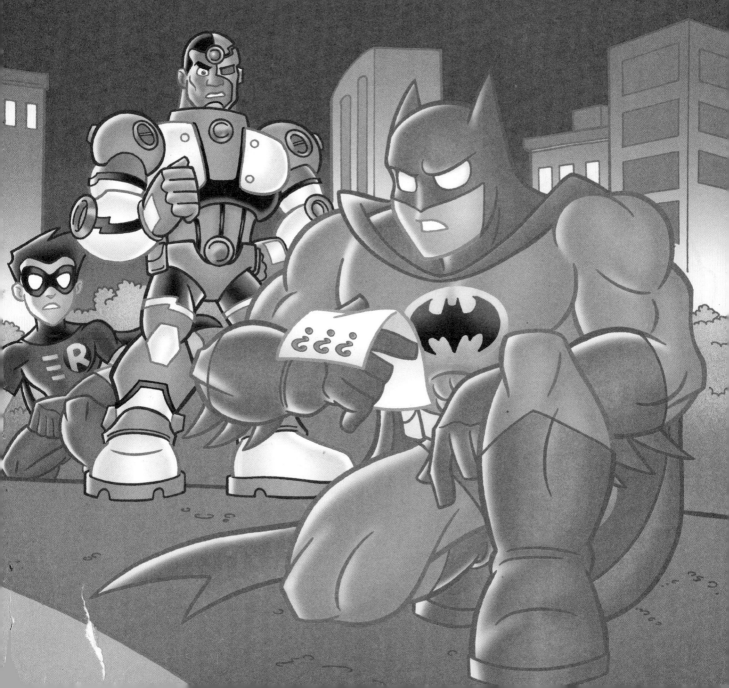

"I'm not sure, but I think I found a clue," said Batman. "It says, 'Riddle me this: One a day keeps the doctor away, but also leads to tooth decay.'"

"What does that mean?" Robin asked.

"An apple a day keeps the doctor away," Cyborg said.

"But apples are good for you," Robin replied.

"Unless they're—"

"Candy apples!" Cyborg exclaimed.

"And the best place to find candy apples is the Gotham City Carnival, which just opened!" Batman said. "Let's go!"

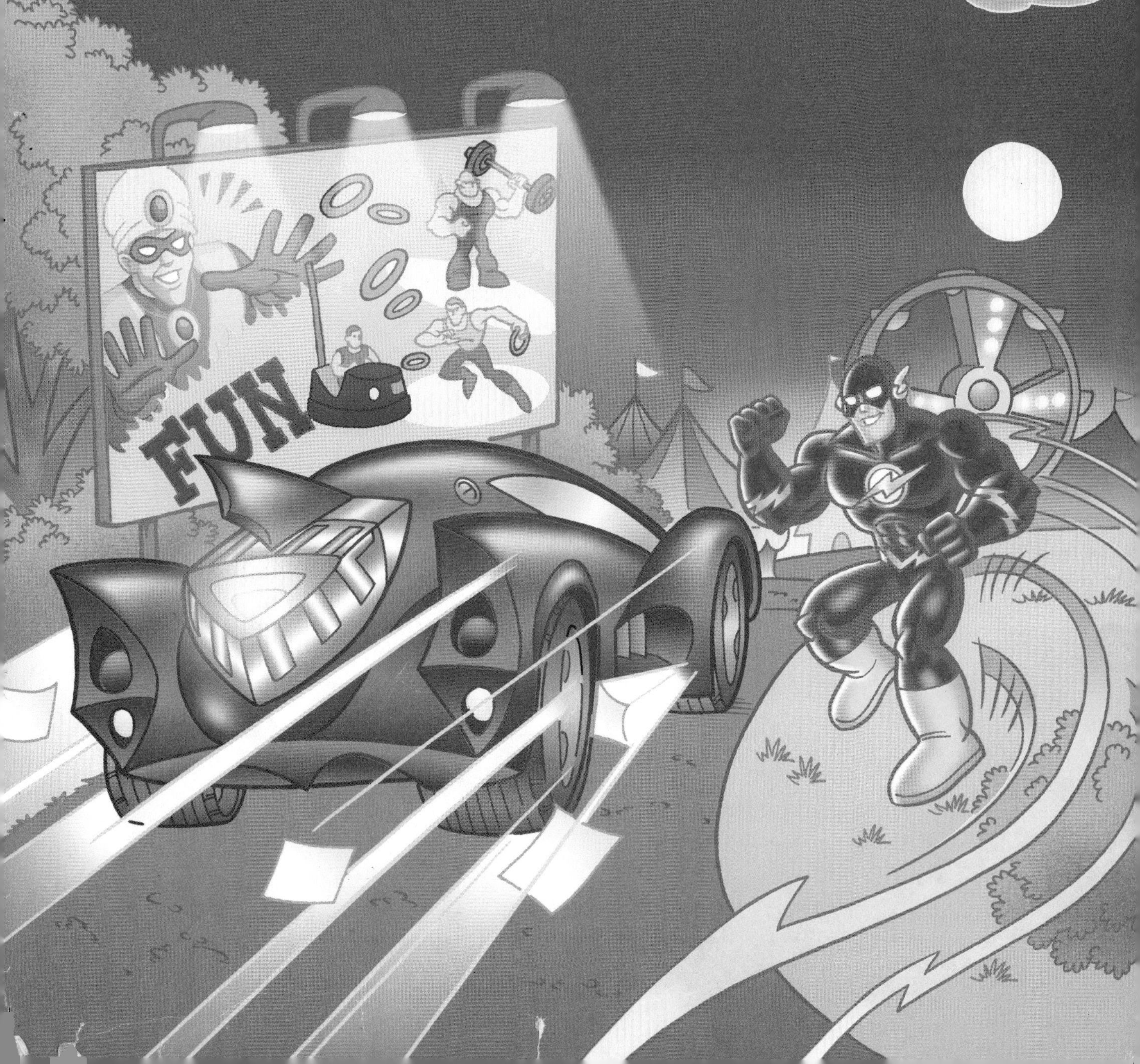
FUN

When Batman and the other Super Friends arrived, the carnival was dark and quiet.
"Where is everybody?" the Flash asked.
"This place should be filled with people," Cyborg added.

"Let's see if this mechanical fortune-teller knows," Batman said, dropping a coin into the slot.

The machine lit up, and a voice said, "To find your friends, riddle me this: I'm exactly the same as you, but always your opposite."

"That's easy," Robin shouted. "A reflection!"

"Quick, everyone—to the House of Mirrors!" Batman said.

At the House of Mirrors, Batman and the others found Green Lantern, Superman, and Aquaman—but something was wrong. They were as still as statues!

A voice boomed over the loudspeaker. "Your friends have been mesmerized by the power of my mirror-amplified light show. Just look into my eyes, and you will be, too!"

"Everyone spread out!" Cyborg shouted. "And whatever you do . . .

. . . don't look into those lights!"

"Ha! You cannot escape my power!" the mysterious voice cried. "Soon you will all do my bidding! Aquaman, Superman, Green Lantern—bring the rest of the Super Friends to me!"

"Keep them busy," Batman said. "I'll find a way to break this hypnotic hold!"

The hypnotized Aquaman tossed steel rings at Robin, but the Boy Wonder was too quick. He dodged and dove through all the deadly circles.

"You'll have to do better than that if you want to win a prize," Robin said.

Green Lantern chased the Flash in his glowing green bumper car. He smashed everything he ran into as he zigzagged through the carnival.

"It's time to find a soft place for you to crash," the Flash said. "And there it is!"

The Flash headed straight for the cotton candy stand—and turned at the very last second. Green Lantern smashed right into the soft, sticky stuff.

"No time for a sweet treat," the Flash said. "Cyborg needs my help!"

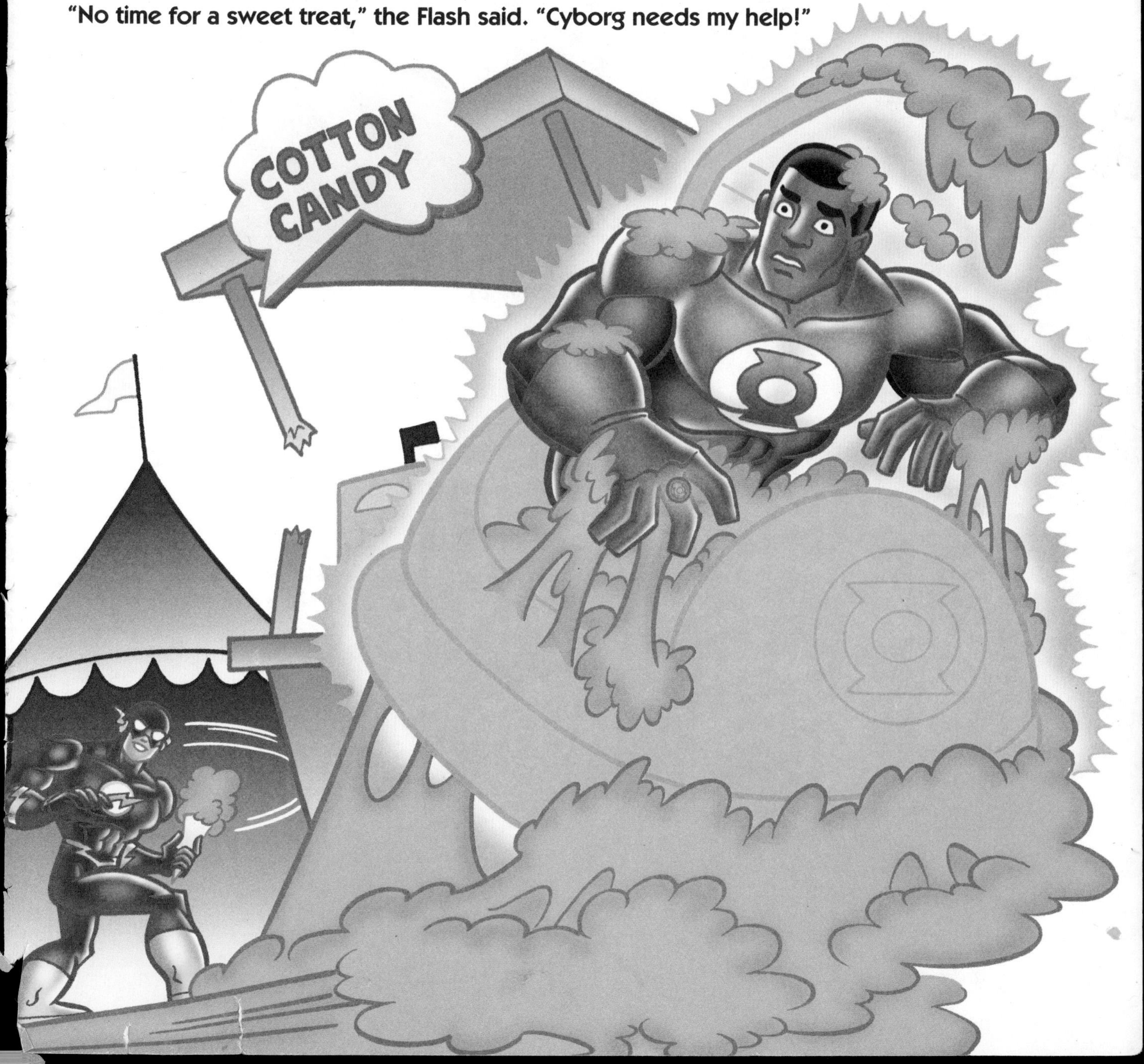
COTTON CANDY

Meanwhile, Cyborg was not having an easy time with Superman.

"He's strong and fast," Cyborg said. "I hope Batman finds a way to snap Superman out of it soon, or he's going to bend me out of shape like a carnival pretzel!"

"He's still not as fast as I am," the Flash said,
running by in a blur and taking the heavy barbell right
out of Superman's hands. "Now it's your turn, Robin."

Just then, Robin led Aquaman around the corner. CRASH! Aquaman and Superman bumped right into each other—and became totally tangled in Aquaman's steel rings. "Those rings won't hold Superman for long," Cyborg said.

"They won't have to, if my plan works," Batman said. "Cyborg, how hard do you think you can ring the Strength Tester bell?"

Cyborg grinned and picked up a hammer. He knew just what Batman had in mind.

"Cover your ears!" Cyborg shouted as he swung the hammer over his head. CLANG! The bell rang so loudly that the sound waves shattered all the glass in the House of Mirrors!

Without the mirrors to magnify the mesmerizing power of the Fun House lights, Superman, Aquaman, and Green Lantern were released from the hypnotic spell!

"And now I think it's about time to bring this carnival caper to a close," Batman said. "Isn't that right, Riddler?" Batman reached into the mechanical fortune-teller and pulled the Riddler from his hiding place.

"Riddle me this," Superman said. "What's easy for a criminal to get into, but hard to get out of?"

"Jail," the Riddler replied sadly.

"That's right," Superman said. "And you are going there for a long time—after you sweep up all this glass."

"Hey, guys, riddle me this," the Flash said. "What's green and pink and sticks to everything?"
"That's easy," Batman replied, and then all the Super Friends said in unison, "Green Lantern!"